KIDS' SPORTS STORIES

TAE KWON DO TEST

by Cristina Oxtra

illustrated by Amanda Erb

PICTURE WINDOW BOOKS
a capstone imprint

Kids' Sports Stories is published by Picture Window Books, an imprint of Capstone.
1710 Roe Crest Drive, North Mankato, Minnesota 56003
www.capstonepub.com

Library of Congress Cataloging-in-Publication Data is available
on the Library of Congress website.
ISBN 978-1-5158-4806-6 (library binding)
ISBN 978-1-5158-5878-2 (paperback)
ISBN 978-1-5158-4807-3 (eBook PDF)

Summary: Mina has all the skills it takes to pass her upcoming yellow belt test in Tae Kwon Do with flying colors. However, a fellow student's recent disappointment shakes her confidence and tempts her to quit.

Designer: Ted Williams

Printed in the United States of America.
PA100

TABLE OF CONTENTS

Chapter 1
A GOOD STUDENT 5

Chapter 2
TEST TROUBLES 12

Chapter 3
MINA TO THE MAX 18

Glossary

ap chagi (AP-CHA-GEE)— a front snap kick

dolyo chagi (DOHL-YO-CHA-GEE)— a roundhouse kick

kihap (KEE-HAP)—a yell

poomse (POOM-SAY)— forms in Tae Kwon Do; poomse are made of set patterns of movements

Tae Kwon Do—a Korean sport that began as self-defense and a way to train one's body and mind

A GOOD STUDENT

Mina was learning a Korean sport called Tae Kwon Do. She wore a white belt with her uniform. White was for beginning students. Mina dreamed of earning a yellow belt. She practiced often and listened closely to her instructor.

"Mina, show me your front snap kick,"
said Master Yoon. "*Ap chagi.*"

Master Yoon held out a hand target.

Mina kicked the target ten times. She
yelled with each kick. "Heeyah!"

"Good kicks and loud *kihaps*," said Master
Yoon.

"Thanks, ma'am," Mina said.

"Now show me your roundhouse kicks,"
said Master Yoon. "*Dolyo chagi*."

Mina turned her body to one side. She kicked the target ten times. Again she yelled with each kick.

"Great," Master Yoon said. "Let me see your *poomse*."

Mina moved her arms and legs the correct way.

Finally, Master Yoon held a soft foam board in front of Mina. Mina balled up her fist and hit the board hard.

"Heeyah!" Mina yelled.

"Good job!" said Master Yoon. "You are ready for your yellow belt test on Friday."

"Yes!" Mina said, a big smile on her face.

"At the test you will do everything you just showed me," Master Yoon said. "There will be one difference, though. You'll have to hit a wooden board, not a foam board."

"I think I can do that," said Mina.

"I know you can," Master Yoon said.
"Stay focused and do your best. Give your
maximum effort."

"Yes, ma'am, I will," Mina said.

Chapter 2

TEST TROUBLES

After class, Mina saw her friend Leo. The two of them had started Tae Kwon Do at the same time, but Leo's skills had grown faster than Mina's. He was sure to earn his yellow belt soon.

"Leo, you're late. Class is over," Mina said.

"I'm here to watch my brother in the next class," said Leo. "My hand is still sore from testing last week."

"You got hurt?" Mina asked.

"I didn't hit the board right the first time," Leo said.

"Oh. Did you try again?" said Mina.

"No. I should've kept trying, but I stopped," said Leo.

"I hope you'll be back in class soon," Mina said.

Leo nodded. "I will. And I'll test again. I'm just not ready yet," he said.

Mina was quiet on the ride home. Her parents asked her what was wrong. She told them she did not want to take the yellow belt test.

"Why? You've been practicing and doing so well," her dad said.

Mina told them what happened to Leo. "I'm afraid to get hurt," she said. "Leo is so much better than I am. If he can't pass the test, I can't!"

"What did Master Yoon say about Friday's test?" her mom asked.

"She told me to stay focused and give my maximum effort," said Mina.

"Then take it to the max, Mina," her dad said. "You can do it!"

Chapter 3

MINA TO THE MAX

Soon it was testing day. Mina stood at the edge of the mat with her parents. Tears filled her eyes.

"I don't want to go," Mina said. "I can't."

"Yes, you can," her mom said with a hug.

Master Yoon called all testing students.
Mina's dad patted his daughter's shoulder.
With wobbly legs, Mina stepped onto the
mat. Testing began.

Mina punched with power. She kicked and yelled. "Heeyah!" she shouted over and over again. Each time she yelled, she felt better and stronger.

Her form was perfect. She moved her arms and legs correctly. Mina was almost done. All she had left was the wooden board.

Mina stared at it. She thought about Leo and his hurt hand. Her stomach flipped. Her heart pounded. Sweat trickled down her face.

Mina turned to the crowd. Her parents
waved. Leo gave her a thumbs up.

Mina looked at the board again and took a deep breath. Then she yelled and hit the board with her fist.

The board didn't break.

Her hand wasn't hurt, but Mina felt shaky. She wanted to stop.

The other students began to cheer.

"Come on, Mina!" they shouted.

Leo yelled, "Don't give up, Mina!"

Master Yoon said, "You can do it,

Mina. Maximum effort, remember?"

Mina tightened her fist and raised it high over her head. With all of her strength and her loudest "HEEYAH!," she brought it down. *OOMPH!*

CRACK! The board split in two.

Everyone clapped and cheered. Mina had passed her test!

At the belt ceremony later, Mina bowed and thanked Master Yoon. She took off her white belt. She watched her instructor tie the new one around her waist. Mina was no longer a beginner. She was now a proud yellow belt.

MINA'S BANANA MILK

Mina celebrated her yellow belt with this popular Korean drink. Ask an adult to help you make it!

What You Need:
- 1 ripe banana, peeled and sliced
- 1½ cups milk
- 1 teaspoon honey
- ¼ teaspoon vanilla extract
- dash of nutmeg

Combine all ingredients in a blender. Blend until smooth.

REPLAY IT

Take another look at this illustration. Mina had just failed to break the board on her first try. Master Yoon was ready for her to try again. How do you think Mina felt right then? What do you think she saw and heard before she hit the board again?

Now pretend you're Mina. Write a note to Leo to tell him how you felt before and after your second try.

ABOUT THE AUTHOR

Cristina Oxtra is the author of *Stephen Hawking: Get to Know the Man Behind the Theory* and *Stan Lee: Get to Know the Comics Creator*. She earned an MFA in creative writing for children and young adults from Hamline University. Cristina and her son train and compete in Tae Kwon Do.

ABOUT
THE ILLUSTRATOR

Amanda Erb is an illustrator from Maryland currently living in the Boston, Massachusetts, area. She earned a BFA in illustration from Ringling College of Art and Design. In her free time, she enjoys playing soccer, learning Spanish, and discovering new stories to read.